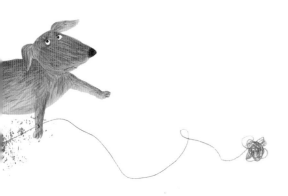

BAD DOG, MACY!

First Published 2018
Printed in China by Toppan Leefung Printing (Shanghai) Co., Ltd.
No. 106 Qingda Road, Pudong, New Area, Shanghai, 201201, China

Thank you to Courtney Chow, Qinfang Gao and Marlo Garnsworthy (in alphabetical order) who were involved in translating and editing this book.

Our thanks also go out to Elyse Williams for her creative efforts in preparing this edition for publication.

# BAD DOG, MACY!

Written by Wenjun QIN
Illustrated by Yinzhi QIN

Macy the dog knocked over Mommy's makeup case! In an instant, pink, red, and purple powder flew everywhere.

"Bad dog, Macy!" Mommy growled.

Without a trace of a smile, Mommy hurriedly took Macy out.

As they crossed the busy streets, Macy wondered, "Where are we going?"

A pleasant melody played in the street. The sweet aroma of ice cream, Macy's favorite honey ice cream, wafted on the breeze. Macy couldn't help but sniff the air.

Mommy led Macy into a store he'd never been in before. He followed Mommy closely. She was the one he trusted and loved the most.

Many dogs were inside, big dogs and small dogs. Most worrying was that Macy didn't know a single one! Macy spied a small dog trembling in a corner. He was wet and covered in scars.

Macy turned to look for Mommy, but she was gone.

"So, you've been left here, too, huh?" a big dog whispered to Macy. "It's horrible here. Look at that little dog. He's suffered a lot."

Don't you know the little dog's mommy doesn't want him anymore?

Why are you so sad?

I've been abandoned.

Suddenly, a woman walked over to them, with strange instruments in her large hands. She picked up another dog and left.

Macy didn't dare make a sound. He shrank backward and huddled with the little dog. The big dog did the same.

Sharing their fear, the three dogs soon became friends.

The woman returned with a
cute Bichon in her arms.

Not long after, the Bichon's mommy
came to pick her up. She even received
a new pair of shoes. Oh, Macy and his
new friends were so envious!

In each other's company, Macy and his friends were no longer as timid.

A Yorkshire terrier ran to her mommy and happily jumped into the car for a ride.

Macy felt relieved. "Everything will be fine," he thought. "All of us will soon be enjoying the sunshine, the moonlight, and the chirping of birds!"

One after another, dogs were picked up.
Soon there remained only Macy and his two friends.

The woman came over. "Who's first?" she asked.

The three dogs looked at each other, now terribly scared again.

The woman reached for the big dog, but he clung on to the table leg.

The little dog retreated, trembling.

Finally, Macy bravely stepped forward, as if to say, "I'll go!"

The woman placed Macy into a warm tub of water. She gave Macy a massage and brushed his fur. After the bath, she put him inside a box to dry. To his surprise, Macy felt quite comfortable.

After Macy's hair was dry, the woman gave him a fresh haircut and trimmed his nails.

After seeing what Macy had gone through, the two other dogs were no longer afraid.

The dogs stared at their new looks. "Now you all look and smell good!" the woman exclaimed.

It was getting dark, and they all missed their mommies. They began sharing memories of their homes.

The big dog's favorite time was after dinner when his mommy turned on the TV and sat on the sofa, while he relaxed on his cushion. Then late at night, his mommy would treat him with midnight snacks.

While they were chatting happily, the big dog's mommy came. The big dog had to say goodbye.

The little dog told Macy that he used to be kept on a windy balcony. That's how he got his scars. Later his mommy had taken him in, and he was even allowed to stay inside. He was now loved.

Suddenly, they heard footsteps outside.

It was the little dog's mommy.

The little dog ran around her. He was crazy with delight.

Now only Macy was left.
He lay quietly by the door.

His two friends were probably happily
at home, but he was all alone. He
began to blame himself. Why did he
have to knock over Mommy's favorite
makeup case?

Macy blamed himself for being naughty and impatient. He was such a bad dog. Mommy must not love him anymore.

Mommy had always been so good to him. She gave him a warm blanket and warm milk in winter, and watermelon juice in summer.

Macy curled up in a corner, feeling chilly.

Suddenly, the door opened.

It was Mommy! She wore a new dress and looked much prettier. In her hand was his favorite ice cream.

He hadn't been abandoned!

On their way home, Macy enjoyed the ice cream while Mommy cuddled him tightly.

What an eventful day it had been!

# THE STORY OF MACY

By Wenjun Qin

Appealing stories often originate from life, some from authors' personal experiences.

Sara, Nick, Xiao Lai, and Xiao Wang. These are all names of dogs I have known — some my own, others my neighbors' or friends' dogs. I enjoyed feeding them and watching them gobble up food. I will never forget the pleasant moments I have spent with my lively and adorable doggy friends.

Among all the dogs I have known, Macy was the most special. When I first met Macy in Wuxi, I immediately felt a bond with him. He was naughty but loyal, innocent but smart. I was always talking about Macy, so I decided to write a story about him.

In Bad Dog, Macy!, Macy makes a mistake and is then sent to a strange place, where he meets new friends. When he is finally reunited with his mommy, he has become a much more mature dog.

I believe that when children read Macy's story, they will be able to step into the story and become friends with Macy. They will feel Macy's love for his family and friends. Any child nurtured with love will have a chance at a splendid future and live a courageous life.

## THE AUTHOR

Wenjun Qin was born in Shanghai, China, in 1954. She is a famous Chinese children's book writer, having won over 50 awards in China and abroad. In 2009, she became the first Chinese writer to be shortlisted for the Astrid Lindgren Memorial Award. She was nominated for the 2002 Hans Christian Andersen Award. She has published 58 children's books and written more than 6 million words. To her, being a children's book author is the world's best job. She has a great understanding of what her readers like.

# MY ENCOUNTER WITH MACY

By Yinzhi Qin

In the city, we often come across dogs, of different sizes and breeds, being walked by their owners. We tend to give cute dogs more glances and play with playful dogs. However, we might not think about their life stories or what the world is like through their eyes.

After I received this story, I asked myself: Is the world black and white in the eyes of a dog? Is their relationship with their owner merely one between a master and their pet, or is there a deeper emotional attachment? After thinking about these questions, I decided to use pencil and acrylic to illustrate. Pencil was perfect for clear and detailed drawings, while acrylic paint was a visual treat for readers.

In order to capture real life in my illustrations, I took a tour along the lanes of Shanghai with a camera in my hands. I took photos of people walking in a hurry and different dogs in pet shops. My illustrations soon formed clearly in my mind.

I paid special attention to detail in my illustrations, like the texture of the road and the wall. I also emphasized the change in Macy's facial expression and mood, so that they would match the story's development.

Illustrating this book was arduous and tedious, but it has brought me so much happiness and satisfaction.

## THE ILLUSTRATOR

Yinzhi Qin currently lives in Shanghai. She graduated from the Department of Chinese Traditional Painting, College of Fine Arts, Shanghai University. She is an art director at a Chinese publishing house. She has illustrated many children's picture books, and her works have won many awards, such as the China National Illustration Award, Bing Xin Children Book Award, East China Book Design Award, and the Award for the Most Beautiful Book in China.